THE
BIG
TIME

ARIANA GRANDE

LAURA K. MURRAY

CREATIVE EDUCATION

ARIANA GRANDE

TABLE OF CONTENTS

MEET ARIANA

Drums beat. Lights flash. Ariana sings and dances for the camera. She swings her long ponytail. Soon, millions of people will see her music video!

riana Grande is an actress and singer. She sings music with catchy beats. She has fans around the world! They watch her on TV. They sing along to her music.

....

Ariana's biggest fans call themselves "Arianators."

ARIANA'S CHILDHOOD

Ariana was born June 26, 1993, in Boca Raton, Florida. She has an older half-brother named Frankie. Ariana's parents split up when she was about eight.

Ariana with her mom and brother in 2011.

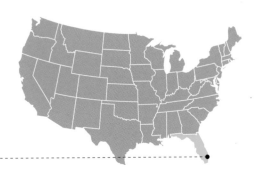

BOCA RATON, FLORIDA

GETTING INTO SINGING

Ariana began singing and acting at an early age. She sang at concerts and sporting events. She helped start a singing group to raise money for people in need. She was in *musicals*, too.

Ariana liked going to see musicals with friends.

At age 15, Ariana got a part on *Broadway*! She won an award for her work. Ariana wanted to do more acting.

· ·

Ariana (center) worked on the musical 13 in 2008.

THE BIG TIME

In 2009, Ariana tried out for a TV show. She was *cast* as Cat Valentine on *Victorious*. The popular Nickelodeon show ended in 2013. Then Ariana starred in the show *Sam & Cat* until 2014.

. . . .

One of Ariana's nicknames is "Little Red."

Ariana kept singing, too. Her first album, *Yours Truly*, came out in 2013. It was a hit! Her next album was *My Everything* in 2014. It reached the top of the music **charts**. Ariana sang with Justin Bieber, The Wanted, Iggy Azalea, and other famous people.

. . . .

Ariana and Little Big Town sang "Bang Bang" at the Country Music Awards in 2014.

OFF THE STAGE

When she is not performing, Ariana likes going to the beach. She spends time with her six dogs. She reads books and watches scary movies.

....

Ariana travels a lot for work and helps animals get adopted.

WHAT IS NEXT?

Ariana went on tour in 2015. She planned to keep acting on TV. Ariana's fans can't wait for her next song!

Ariana performed at the 2015 NBA All-Star Game (left) and at the 57th Grammy Awards (right).

WHAT ARIANA SAYS ABOUT ...

ANIMALS

"I love animals more than I love most people, not kidding."

BEING YOURSELF

"Don't ever doubt yourselves or waste a second of your life. It's too short, and you're too special."

SINGING AT THE WHITE HOUSE

"My throat dried up. I was right in front of [president Barack Obama], and I thought, 'How am I going to get through this?'"

GLOSSARY

Broadway a street in New York City famous for its plays

cast chosen to play a part

charts the popular ratings of music

musicals plays in which the characters sing a lot

WEBSITES

Ariana Grande
http://www.arianagrande.com/
This is Ariana's own website, with news, pictures, and videos.

Ariana Grande Biography
http://www.billboard.com/artist/1484343/ariana-grande/biography
This site tells about Ariana's life and music.

READ MORE

Gagne, Tammy. *Ariana Grande*. Hockessin, Del.: Mitchell Lane, 2016.

Tieck, Sarah. *Ariana Grande: Famous Actress & Singer*. Minneapolis: Abdo, 2015.

INDEX

PUBLISHED BY Creative Education
P.O. Box 227, Mankato, Minnesota 56002
Creative Education is an imprint of The Creative Company
www.thecreativecompany.us

DESIGN AND PRODUCTION BY Christine Vanderbeek
ART DIRECTION BY Rita Marshall
PRINTED IN the United States of America

PHOTOGRAPHS BY Alamy (epa european pressphoto agency b.v., WENN Ltd), Corbis (Mario Anzuoni/Reuters, BleacherCreatures.tv/Splash News, Rick Friedman, Machete/Splash News, Walter McBride, Jason Moore/ZUMA Press, Kento Nara/Geisler-Fotopress/dpa, SartorialPhoto/Splash News, Splash News/Splash News), Getty Images (Neilson Barnard/Staff), iStockphoto (colevineyard, Pingebat), Shutterstock (s_buckley)

LIBRARY OF CONGRESS CATALOGING-IN-PUBLICATION DATA
Murray, Laura K.
Ariana Grande / Laura K. Murray.
p. cm. — (The big time)
Includes index.
Summary: An elementary introduction to the life, work, and popularity of Ariana Grande, an American pop singer and actress known for her work on kid's shows and such songs as "Bang Bang."

ISBN 978-1-60818-669-3 (HARDCOVER)
ISBN 978-1-56660-705-6 (EBOOK)
1. Grande, Ariana. 2. Singers—Biography. I. Title.
ML3930.G724M87 2016
782.42164092—dc23 [B]   2015026253

CCSS: RI.1.1, 2, 3, 4, 5, 6, 7; RI.2.1, 2, 5, 6, 7; RI.3.1, 5, 7, 8; RI.4.3, 5; RF.1.1, 3, 4; RF.2.3, 4

FIRST EDITION   9 8 7 6 5 4 3 2 1